P9-DDS-828

A New Home for TOBY

Written By Jean Eick
Illustrated By Atilio Pernisco

Written By Jean Eick
Illustrated By Atilio Pernisco

ISBN-13 978-1-60068-210-0

Second Printing, May 2009

Distributed by Wholesale Resort Accessories, Inc.
12116 Chandelle Way, Suite D
Truckee, CA 96161

© Impact, Designed & Distributed in the U.S.A. Printed in China

"Toby, stop chasing butterflies and eat your breakfast now!"
Mother bear was not happy to see her little cub playing instead of eating.
But Toby was having too much fun in the beautiful summer
sunshine at Lake Tahoe.

He liked running and playing. He did not like bees.
And he did not like to reach in for the honey even though it tasted so sweet.
So instead, Toby crawled to a manzanita bush
and started munching on the berries.

As Toby started eating, his mother stood up on her back legs.
He quickly ran over to the nearest tree and climbed as high as he could in record speed.
That should make Mother happy, he thought!
So he called out to her, "Did you see how fast I made it up the tree, Mother?"

Now his mother was really annoyed.
"Toby, how many times have I told you that when you are up in the tree it is because danger is near? You must stay still and be quiet!"
She shook her head. This playful little cub was not learning about the dangers in the forest.

But before Mother finished scolding Toby, the forest by the lake was alive with animals running! Mother called to Toby, "Come down now Toby. We need to leave."

He could hear the fear in his mother's voice and quickly climbed to the ground. Now Toby could smell smoke. It was very strong.

"FIRE!" yelled his mother. "We need to run fast Toby." Toby and his mother began to run through the woods. They ran and ran.

As they ran over an alpine creek in the forest, Toby could feel the cold water on his hot little paws.
He wanted to stop and rest for awhile. Mother urged him on.
"No Toby, we must not stop until we are safely out of the path of the fire."
So they kept going all day long.

Finally, as evening was approaching, they stopped. By this time Toby was very hungry and hot from running. His short legs ached. Toby knew by now that they must be a long, long way from home. Mother helped him find a nice Manzanita bush to munch on.

"When are we going back to our den?" Toby whispered to his mother.
"We will have to find a new home now Toby. All of our food will be gone. We must now find another den before winter." His mother sounded sad.
Toby was sad too.
The next morning Toby and his mother started on their journey to find a new home.

Before long, they came upon a small lake. Toby quickly jumped in.

"Oh Mother, this will be a great place to live," Toby called from the lake.

"No, Toby, we cannot live here. It is too close to people." Mother responded sternly as she watched Toby playing in the water. Toby could tell that his mother did not like people.

After a brief rest, Toby and his mother continued on through the forest. Soon they could hear a strange noise. As he was about to ask Mother what was making the noise, Toby could see a big boat coming into a bay down on Lake Tahoe.

Toby was frightened by the noise the big boat made. Mother quickly told Toby, "It's okay. Let's go down a little closer so you can see the boat

"Okay Toby," Mother called back as she started walking.
"I want you to stay right behind me now. Do not stop, unless I do."
They were alongside a busy road. Mother waited until she did not see any cars.
Then she started across the road. Toby stayed right behind her.

Suddenly, a car was racing down the road.

"Run Toby!" Mother yelled.

Toby ran as fast as his little legs would let him go. As he reached the other side of the road, his mother let out a sigh of relief.

Toby had made it in time!

Toby and his mother watched the boat for awhile before going back into the forest. Then they traveled for several more days.

Every night Mother would find a
safe place for them to spend the night.
And each time she would tell Toby that it
was not a good place for their new home.

Then one day they came to some huge rocks alongside Lake Tahoe. Toby liked climbing on the rocks and feeling the warm sun.

He also liked being up close to the giant lake. It was so blue and it sparkled in the sunshine. Toby hoped that this would be their new home.

Toby sat down to take a short nap on one of the big rocks.
Then, Mother stood up! Toby quickly ran up a nearby tree.
This time he quietly watched from above
and saw some people in uniforms.
They were looking right at his mother!

Before Mother could run away, one of the men shot something at her! She fell to the ground. "Oh no," Toby wanted to scream out. But he remembered Mother telling him that he must always be very quiet when hiding in a tree from danger.

Toby watched as the people put his mother in a big net and pulled her to a truck with a cage on the back of it.

Mother was still not moving when they drove away.

Toby stayed up in the tree until it was dark and the stars were shining overhead. He was alone and hungry. He cried for awhile and then decided to climb down from the tree.
As he started looking around for food, a little raccoon came by.

"Are you okay Toby?" The raccoon asked. "I heard what happened to your mother."

"I'm hungry" Toby told the little raccoon.

"Well," said the raccoon, "we are just going to get some food. Why don't you come along with us?"

Toby thought about it for a minute, and since he was really hungry decided it would be okay for him to go with the raccoons.

NO PARKING
They took him to a small brown building with a huge garbage container behind it.
Toby knew immediately that his mother would not like this place. She always told Toby never to eat garbage.
But Toby was really hungry and he could smell food. So he decided to eat a little and then go back.

The raccoons jumped right into the garbage container!
Before Toby could get in, he heard yelling and screaming.
People! Toby started running again.
He ran all the way back to the tree where his mother had left him.
He climbed up and stayed there all night long.
He was very frightened, cold and hungry. He cried himself to sleep.
NO PARKING

When the sun came up in the morning,
Toby was so hungry that his stomach was growling.

Again he started to cry.
But as he looked around from high up in the tree he could see it was safe to climb down.

Toby started looking around when a little squirrel came by.
He asked, "Are you looking for some nuts?"
"Oh yes," Toby replied. "I am really hungry."
"Well," continued the little squirrel,
"right over by that bush, are lots and lots of acorns."
Toby didn't even wait to thank the little squirrel.
Instead he raced over to the bush where the
ground was covered with acorns.

Toby liked the acorns.
He ate and ate.
Before long he was no longer hungry.

Then he remembered that he was still alone.
He sat down wondering what he should do now.
He remembered what Mother had said.
She had told Toby that if they were ever separated,
he should stay where she had left him.
She would come back and find him.

So Toby waited for several days. Now the acorns were almost gone.
But as he was starting to cry again, he heard a noise in the forest.
Quickly Toby raced up the tree.
Maybe those people in uniforms were coming back to get him.
Toby was so scared that he closed his eyes.

After a minute, he decided to take a peek.
As he looked down, he saw his mother!
Mother looked up and saw Toby.
Toby raced down to greet her.

As they hugged and hugged,
Mother said "Toby, I am so happy that you remembered to stay here."

Then she told Toby that the people took her into the forest and left her there.
But on her way back she found a new home!

Toby couldn't wait to see their new home. So they immediately left the rocks by the lake.

They traveled only a short distance before they came to a beautiful meadow.
It was filled with berries and grass and butterflies!

Beyond the meadow was a hollow tree. Mother had already filled the tree with pine boughs and needles. This was their new home. Toby was so happy he wanted to start chasing butterflies!

So as Toby and his mother climbed into the tree for a nap, snow started to fall. Winter was arriving at Lake Tahoe. Toby and his mother had found their new home just in time!

Lake Tahoe
BEAR
XING
CALIF
8
MS. DIXIE
N
W
E
S

If you are interested in learning more about the bears and Lake Tahoe be sure to get a copy of **Toby's Lake Tahoe Fun Book** or you can contact the following:

Sierra Wild Bears
@Sierrawildbear.gov

California Department of Fish & Game
1416 Ninth Street
Sacramento, CA 95814
@www.fgc.ca.gov

Nevada Department of Wildlife
1100 Valley Road
Reno, NV 89512
@www.ndow.org.

U. S. Fish & Wildlife Service
2800 Cottage Way Suite 2606
Sacramento, CA 95825
@www.fws.gov/cno

Bear League
P O Box 393
Homewood, CA 96141
@www.savebears.org

The Tahoe Bear Proof Garbage Containers
can be purchased by contacting:
Kmanfredi@earthlink.net